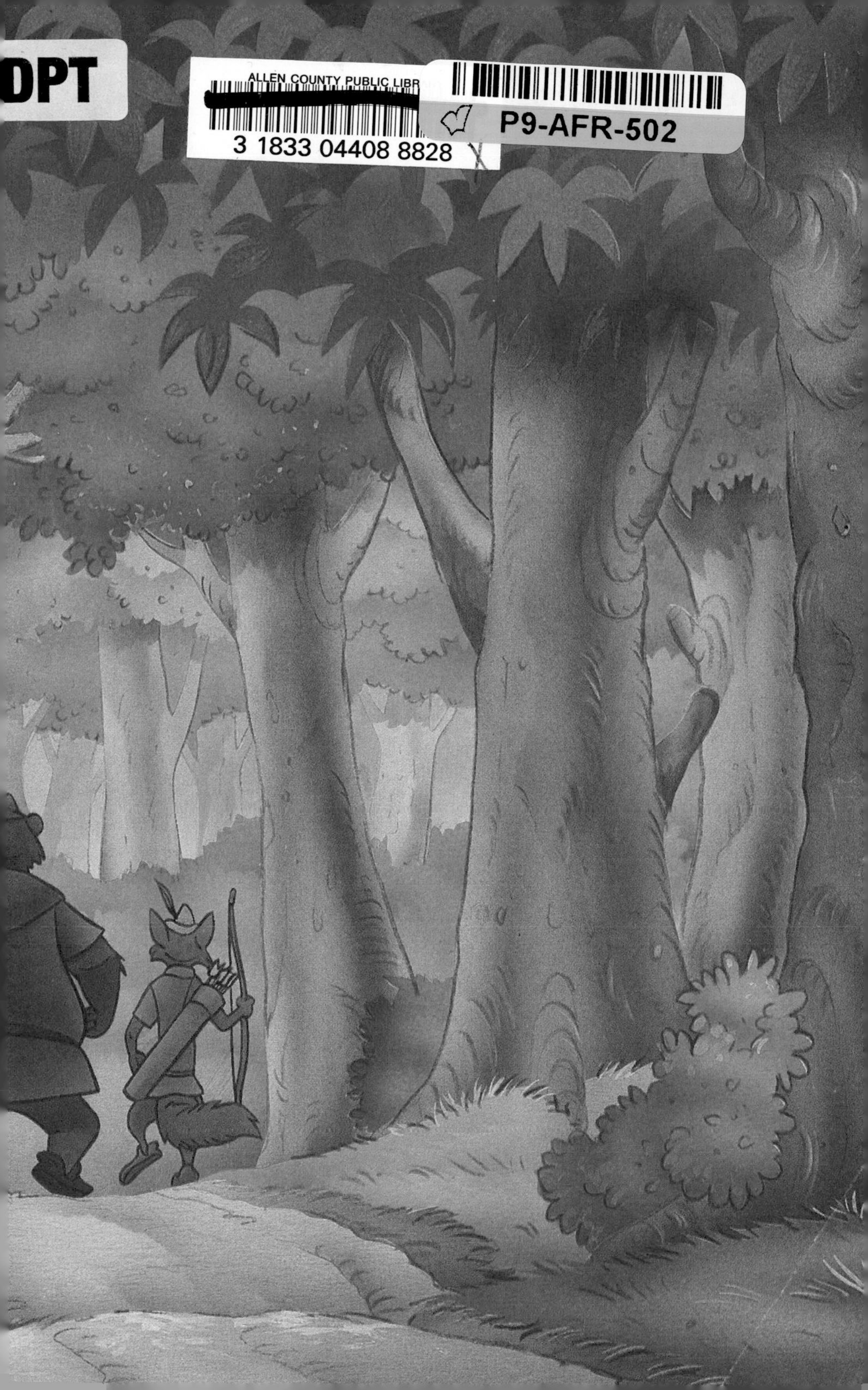

ISBN: 0-7172-8794-7

Manufactured in the United States of America.
A B C D   1 2 3 4

Disney's
Robin Hood
Sends a Message

Once there was a hero named Robin Hood.
He lived in Sherwood Forest with his friends,
Friar Tuck, Little John, and Skippy Bunny.

Robin Hood had an enemy named Prince
John. The wicked prince took money from the
poor people of England, but Robin Hood always
got it back for them.

Far from Sherwood Forest, in Prince John's castle, lived Maid Marian and Lady Kluck. Maid Marian loved Robin Hood. She wished she could see him, but she knew Robin would be arrested if he came near the castle.

"Don't worry, Maid Marian,"
Lady Kluck said. "Robin Hood
will find a way to see you. He
always does."

Lady Kluck was right. Robin Hood
wrote Maid Marian a note asking her
to meet him at the fair.

Robin Hood asked Skippy to deliver the letter. "Don't let anyone see you," he warned his young friend.

"Don't worry!" Skippy cried. And off he went.

When he reached the village, Skippy hid
Robin Hood's letter in his hat. Then he pulled
the hat down over his ears. At dusk he bravely
marched into the castle.

Skippy carefully tiptoed past the sleeping guards to find Maid Marian.

Skippy climbed
up a vine to Maid
Marian's window.

He pulled the letter from his hat and left it for her on the window sill.

But Skippy didn't realize that one of the guards was really awake. And he didn't know the guard saw him leave the letter.

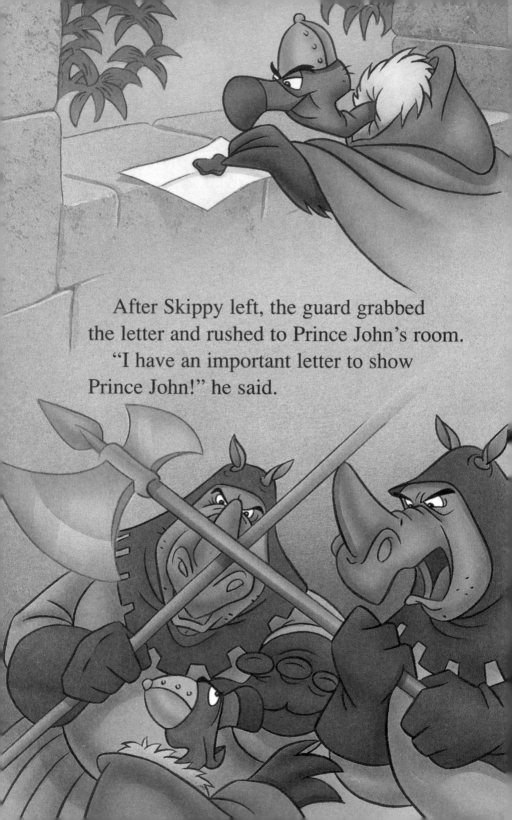

After Skippy left, the guard grabbed
the letter and rushed to Prince John's room.
"I have an important letter to show
Prince John!" he said.

Prince John, his knight Sir Hiss, and the sheriff were busy counting money, but they stopped when they learned that the guard had a letter from Robin Hood.

"What does it say?" Prince John demanded.

The sheriff read the
letter aloud. It said:

Dear Marian,
Please meet me at
the fair tomorrow.
I miss you.
Love, Robin Hood

"At last we can catch Robin Hood!" whispered the sheriff.

"We must be careful!" hissed Sir Hiss. "Robin Hood has tricked us before!"

"Keep quiet, you fool!" shouted Prince John.

So poor Maid Marian never received
Robin Hood's letter. She didn't know he
wanted to see her at the fair. She began to
worry. "Do you think I'll ever see him
again?" she asked Lady Kluck.

Just then there was a knock on the door. "Quick! Hide Robin's picture," Lady Kluck whispered. She knew Prince John would be angry if he saw it.

Lady Kluck opened the door. There stood
Prince John with Sir Hiss.

"Would you dear ladies care to join me at the fair this afternoon?" the sly prince asked. The two ladies were surprised. Prince John never asked them to go anywhere.

"Yes, we'll go," Maid Marian answered.

"Wonderful!" giggled the prince. "We will meet in ten minutes."

Lady Kluck did not trust Prince John
and Sir Hiss. She opened the door and
listened to them talking.

"We are sure to catch Robin Hood this time!" Prince John cried as he skipped down the hall.

Lady Kluck rushed back into the room. She had to warn Robin Hood. She looked out the window and saw Skippy. He was waiting to see if Maid Marian had a message for Robin Hood.

Lady Kluck rushed downstairs to tell
Skippy about the evil prince's plans.
   "Prince John is going to trap Robin
Hood at the fair," Lady Kluck exclaimed.

Skippy ran as fast as he could all the way
to Sherwood Forest. "What's the matter?"
Robin Hood asked him.

Skippy quickly told Robin Hood and
Little John about the prince's plan.

Robin Hood laughed. "We'll see
who will get caught…"
  "…and who will do the catching!"
chuckled Little John. "I have
an idea!"

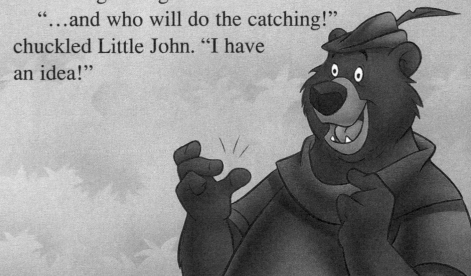

Back at the castle, Prince John and his men were ready to leave for the fair. "Robin Hood has met his match!" roared the prince. "Let's go!" He sent the sheriff and his men on ahead to the fair.

Lady Kluck and Maid Marian joined
the prince in his royal carriage and
they were on their way.

"It should be a very interesting fair,"
Prince John said with an evil grin.
"Yesss," agreed Sir Hiss.
"I'm sure it will be," replied Lady Kluck.

Up ahead, Robin Hood and Little John were waiting. They had tied a big net in the trees.

As Prince John's carriage passed underneath the net, Robin Hood and Little John cut the ropes…

…and down came the net! Prince John
was the one who was caught!

"Now what?"
Prince John roared.

Robin Hood and Little John dashed
out from behind the trees and ran over
to the carriage.

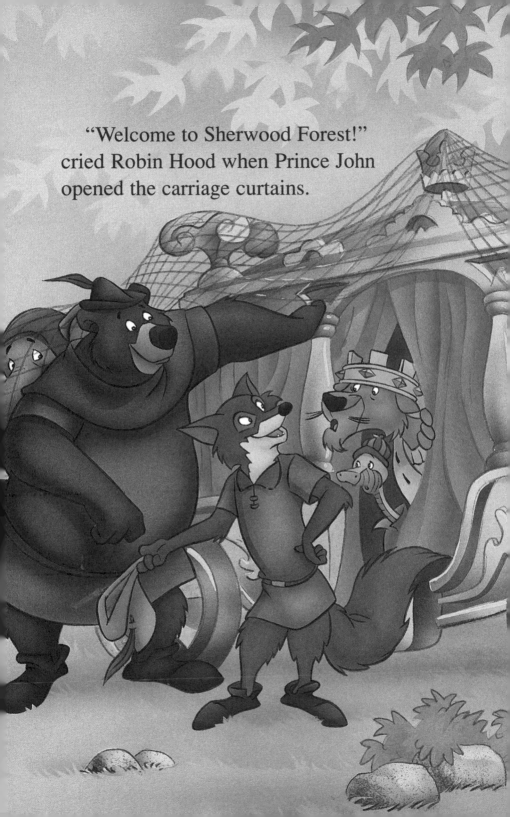

"Welcome to Sherwood Forest!"
cried Robin Hood when Prince John
opened the carriage curtains.

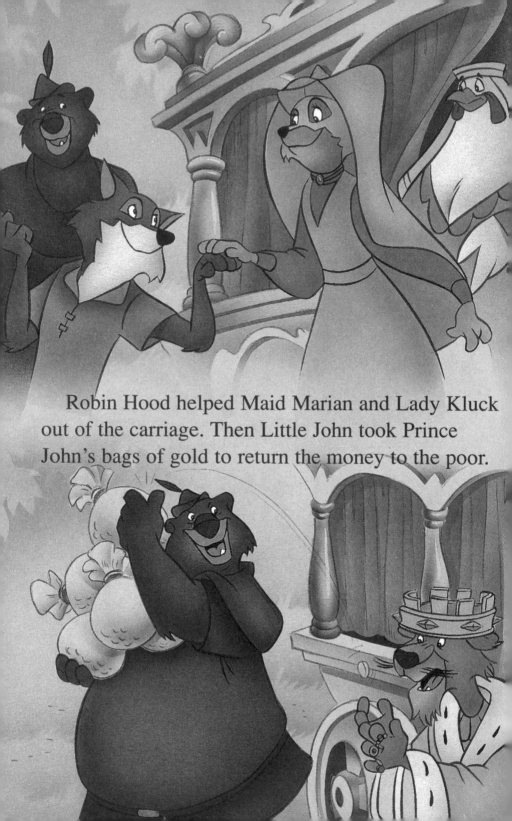

Robin Hood helped Maid Marian and Lady Kluck out of the carriage. Then Little John took Prince John's bags of gold to return the money to the poor.

Soon all the friends of Sherwood Forest
were celebrating Robin Hood's great success
in outsmarting Prince John once more.

Robin Hood bowed to Maid Marian.
"May I have this dance?" he asked.

When Prince John returned to the castle,
the sheriff was waiting for him.

"We've been tricked!" the sheriff cried.
"Robin Hood never turned up at the fair."

"Oh, he turned up," Prince John said. "But not at the fair. And now I don't have Robin Hood—or my bags of gold!" And with that, he put his thumb in his mouth and began to plan a brand new way to catch the hero of Sherwood Forest.

OXFORD MEDICAL PUBLICATIONS

Living with dying
The management of terminal disease

The many-headed dragon of terminal pain. Photograph of a medieval tapestry given to the authors by a patient who said: 'This is what my illness feels like to me'.